Revamp Your Room

Makeover Fun 101™

Kirsten Hall

Scholastic Inc.
New York Toronto London Auckland Sydney
Mexico City New Delhi Hong Kong Buenos Aires

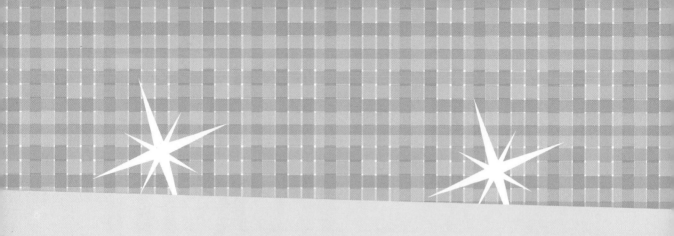

Designed by Emily Muschinske
Illustrated by Karen Wolcott

ISBN 0-439-80296-2

12 11 10 9 8 7 6 5 4 3 2 1   5 6 7 8 9 10/0

Printed in the U.S.A.

First Scholastic printing, September 2005

Come On In

Take a look at yourself in the mirror—not just an "I'm-late-for-school-but-I-just-need-to-quickly-make-sure-this-lip-gloss-matches-my-outfit" glance in the mirror. No, stop and take a *real*, *long* look at yourself.

You've grown up a lot over the last couple of years, haven't you? You're taller. Your feet are bigger. Your face looks older. Your hairstyle is cooler. You're looking good—and, the even more exciting news is that **you're not a little girl anymore**!

Now take a look around your room. While you've been busy changing, your room's pretty much stayed the same. This room is much better suited for the little girl you were a couple of years ago—not the cool, happenin' girl you've recently become!

No reason to worry! Whipping your room into shape is a much easier task than you might realize. In fact, you will see that even some of the smallest and easiest changes will make a huge difference!

So, roll up those sleeves and get ready to revamp your room. You'll be amazed by how extraordinary the ordinary can become—in practically no time at all!

Room Makeover Web Site

For additional makeover fun, get online and check out **www.scholastic.com/makeover**

To log on, type in your first password: **roomrevup**

Each month, you'll get another password to gain access to the next super-fun site! You'll find the password in each upcoming Makeover book.

First Things First

You're probably itching to get started! But before you do so, survey your bedroom and think about what you'd like to do to it. There are three things you should do first:

1. Check It Out!

With a pen and paper in hand, stand in the middle of your room. Slowly turn around in a complete circle. Some things in your room still do look pretty cool, don't they? Take notes as to which things are keepers—try not to concentrate only on the losers! List things in three categories: Keepers, losers, and maybes. Maybes are things you might want to keep—once they're revamped, of course!

2. Talk It Out!

Before you change anything, it's important you ask your parents for permission first. Since part of being the cool new you is being responsible, invite your parents to sit down to discuss your room plans. Explain to them how you're feeling—you're eager to make some changes to your room. Share some of your ideas with them—and let them share theirs, too!

3. Plan It Out!

Think about how much money you will need and try to come up with a budget. Revamping your room doesn't mean everything has to be brand new. But you will need some money for materials—like paint, glue, beads, stickers, and glitter, for example—if you want to make improvements to the things you already have.

> **Note:** Whenever you see this symbol, it means you should ask your parents first before you do the activity. You'll also probably need their help with part of it.

Pay the Piggy!

Once you have a budget, how are you going to get the dough? Think of some ways you can earn money for revamping your room. Baby-sit! Rake leaves! Shovel snow! Store your earnings in one of these adorable piggy banks. Be sure to put one dollar of every two you earn inside of it. Then, watch your room fund grow before your very eyes!

You will need:

- 1 plastic milk, juice, or soda bottle
- Glue
- 4 thread spools
- Scissors
- Various decorations (fabric cut-outs, paper, stickers, pipe cleaners, etc.)

ASK FIRST

Step 1: Glue the four thread spools to the side of the bottle as shown. These will be the pig's legs. Let it dry for one hour.

Step 2: Ask an adult to cut a slit on the pig's "back." It should be large enough for coins and folded bills to fit through (but not your hand!).

Step 3: Use whatever decorations you have on hand to give the pig a face—and any other cute detailing you can think of!

What's Your Style?

We've established that your tastes have changed over the last couple of years. After all, part of growing up is developing your own style. But how would you describe yourself now?

Answer the following multiple-choice questions to find out exactly what kind of stylish girl you've become. Knowing your new look will come in handy as you begin the revamping process!

1. **School has been canceled! You can't wait to:**

   🕶 climb back into bed and finish that great book you're reading.

   👜 surf the Internet for hours while listening to some new CDs.

   👑 throw on a fluffy robe and give yourself a manicure and pedicure.

   🦋 call all your friends while sifting through boxes of old photographs.

   🌸 plant rows of seeds in your new, beautiful flower garden.

   ☀ meet up with some friends and ride bikes/walk around town.

2. **Your idea of an awesome vacation is a visit to:**

   🌸 an exotic island covered in wild and tropical flowers.

   👜 a bustling city where everyone's moving so fast it's a blur.

   👑 a spa where you can be pampered from sunup to sundown.

   🕶 a friend's old cottage where everything is super-comfortable.

   🦋 a private beach where you can chill out and listen to the waves.

   ☀ sports camp for a week so you can get ready for the season.

3. **Your dream boyfriend is someone who:**

   🕶 loves to snuggle in a hammock.

   👑 takes you out for fancy dinners every night.

   ☀ wins your heart with romantic love letters.

   👜 wears super-funky clothes.

   🦋 wants to travel the world with you.

   🌸 has dozens of adorable pets you can play with.

4. There are so many great movies out! The one you desperately want to see is the:

- 👑 love story.
- 🦋 comedy flick.
- ☀️ action film.
- 👜 drama.
- 🌸 documentary.
- 🕶️ horror film.

5. It's your birthday, and you've just opened all your gifts. Without question, your favorite is:

- 👜 the cutting-edge laptop.
- 🌸 the bouquet of twelve long-stem roses.
- 🕶️ the gift card for a local bookstore.
- 👑 the sparkly jewelry set.
- 🦋 the vintage record collection.
- ☀️ the new rollerblades.

6. The quality you like most about yourself is:

- 🕶️ your patience.
- 👜 your honesty.
- 👑 your appearance.
- 🦋 your spontaneity.
- 🌸 your thoughtfulness.
- ☀️ your manners.

7. Your crystal ball sees you in the future as a(n):

- 👑 model or actress.
- 🦋 lawyer or doctor.
- ☀️ archaeologist or scientist.
- 👜 writer or artist.
- 🌸 fashion designer or business owner.
- 🦋 veterinarian or chef.

8. To you, "fantastic footwear" means:

- old bunny slippers.
- platform shoes.
- high, high heels.
- everyday flip-flops.
- preppy penny loafers.
- moccasins.

9. Is that your stomach growling? You sure could go for a(n):

- slice of extra-cheese pizza.
- fruit smoothie.
- cupcake with tons of frosting.
- energy-fuelling protein bar.
- chocolate croissant.
- fruit salad and a scoop of fro-yo.

10. Imagine the world in just one color. It would definitely look best in:

- lime.
- pink.
- silver.
- turquoise.
- lilac.
- gold.

11. Lucky you—you won the lottery! You can't wait to buy:

- a sprawling mansion with an Olympic-size pool.
- flat-screen television sets for everyone you've ever known.
- a fancy yacht to take you on a journey around the world.
- land to turn into an animal sanctuary.
- piles of beautiful diamond jewelry.
- nothing! You'd invest your money and watch it grow!

12. There's no doubt about it— the best kind of music ever invented is:

- techno.
- oldies.
- rock.
- hip-hop.
- country.
- pop.

What's Your Score?

Now check to see which of these six icons matches most of your answers. Exactly what type of stylin' girl are you?

Make sure to visit *all* of the pages in this section, even if their titles don't match your specific personality type. Remember, mixing styles can be loads of fun, too! The only rule that matters when it comes to decorating is a simple one—as long as you like it, it works!

The CHILL Chick

Check out page 10!

Page 11 is all about you!

The Pretty Princess

THE MODERN MAMA

REDIRECT IMMEDIATELY TO PAGE 12!

Time for you to turn to page 13!

THE SUPER PREP

The Flower Girl

Learn more on page 14!

Wander over to page 15!

The Free Spirit

The **CHILL Chick**

STYLE STATS

Favorite fabric: Cotton
Color combo choice: Blue and orange
Style summary: Casual cool
What's doing: Chilling

You're super low-maintenance. You love to spend time just spending time. You write. You read. You listen to mellow tunes. Your style is simple—not sassy. You surround yourself with fluffy pillows and soft colors. The scent of a lavender candle is your idea of heaven. A bubble bath is the next best thing. Your room is your sanctuary.

The Pretty Princess

STYLE STATS

Favorite fabric: Satin
Color combo choice: Pink and more pink!
Style summary: Sitting pretty
What's doing: Primping

Pink is one of your favorite colors, and you love all things girly. You can't get enough fluff. There can never be too many feathers, glitter, fur, or sequins. Hearts make you happy. Photos of your best friends do, too. Life is all about being royally pampered—or pampering yourself, if need be! Your room is your palace.

THE
MODERN
MAMA

STYLE STATS

Favorite fabric: Plastic
Color combo choice: Silver and black
Style summary: Hip and happening
What's doing: Surfing

The world is changing all the time, and you have no problem keeping up with it. You believe that things should be quick and easy. Sleek lines and simplicity work best in your surroundings. It's hard for you to believe that the Internet hasn't been around forever. Electronics rule. Your room is a techie's dream.

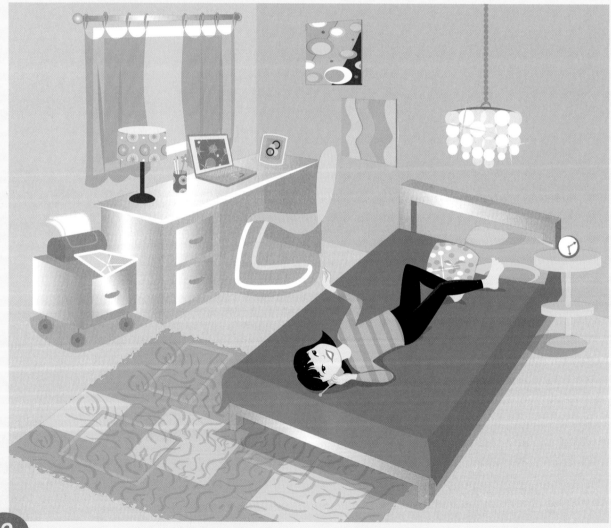

THE SUPER PREP

STYLE STATS

Favorite fabric: Linen
Color combo choice: Navy and cream
Style summary: Everyday elegance
What's doing: Studying

You have traditional taste. Plaid is one of your favorite patterns. You firmly believe that there's a place for everything, and everything must be in that place! You're a fan of items that are tried-and-true—even if someone else might call them "yesterday." For you, life is about quality, not quantity. Your room is timeless.

The Flower Girl

STYLE STATS

Favorite fabric: **Anything organic!**
Color combo choice: **Yellow and green**
Style summary: **Natural**
What's doing: **Gardening**

You love to bring nature inside. If you could spend all of your time with animals, you would. Spring is your favorite season, when everything is in full bloom. You don't let stress wear you down. Life is about remembering to stop and smell the flowers. Your room is your garden.

The Free Spirit

STYLE STATS

Favorite fabric: Faux-suede

Color combo choice: Purple and gold

Style summary: Mix it up

What's doing: Creating

Who said things have to match? Color and style don't concern you. All that matters is whether or not you like it. An old-fashioned blanket looks pretty cool alongside a funky, modern chair. You are the hallmark of cool for hipsters everywhere. Your room is your palette.

Draw It! Then Move It!

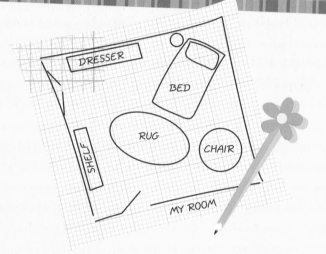

Now you know everything about your style. But you're still not *quite* ready to get started. That's because—as with most things you do in life—you need to make some plans. The results will be that much better if you take the time to sit down and think about them first. So, grab a piece of graph paper and a pencil with an eraser.

Architects and interior designers always make sketches before they get to work. The scaled drawings, or "plans," that they create reflect their visions and allow them to see what will work and what won't—without wasting any time.

You can start by making a floor plan of your room. Take measurements. How long is each wall? Are there any corners you need to be concerned about?

Next, take measurements of your furniture, starting with the biggest pieces—like your bed, dresser, desk, and chair. Now you can start sketching. Which new arrangements will work and which won't? Figuring that out now will save you loads of time later!

TIME-SAVING TIP

Use a formula to convert the measurements you have taken to ones that you can use on your plan. For example, if your bed measures six feet in length, make it six squares long on your graph paper.

16

Get Moving

Moving furniture around to fit your plans is another tough task. You will probably need to enlist help. Thank heavens you have all those cooperative friends and family members!

1. **Move** your bed so its back is against a different wall.

2. **Try** your chair in another corner.

3. **Turn** your desk so it faces a new direction.

4. **Change** the way things are arranged on your desktop or atop your dresser.

5. **Move** a hanging picture from one wall to another.

6. **Ask** a parent to switch your light bulb to a different watt level.

7. **Organize** the books on your shelf in a new order—by size or title.

8. **Switch** your pillows around. Maybe even flip your blanket or comforter.

9. **Turn** your rug so it faces a new angle— maybe even diagonally!

10. **Put** things away! A messy room NEVER looks good—no matter what else you do.

Before

After

Visit
www.scholastic.com/makeover
to make your own super-cool, computerized room plan!

Feng Shui 4-1-1

Did you know that some of today's hottest interior decorators base their room designs on an ancient Chinese approach called *feng shui* (pronounced "fung shway")? The literal translation of feng shui is "wind" and "water." Just as fresh air and water nourish our bodies, the practice of feng shui can actually nourish your room.

Behind the practice of feng shui is something called "chi." Chi means energy. The way that we arrange things in our room will determine how the chi, or energy, flows around us. When things are too cluttered, chi is unable to move freely. As a result, you might feel uncomfortable—tired, frustrated, bored, or even angry.

Feng shui is also known as "the art of placement." Those who subscribe to feng shui think long and hard about where things will go in any given space. Things don't go where they are simply convenient. They are put there for a reason. The overall balance in your room is important. There should never be too much in one area—just as another area should never be neglected.

Good Feng Shui

Bad Feng Shui

You can make changes to your room based on the principles of feng shui, too! Check out the list on the facing page to see how you can make some simple changes in a snap!

Feng Shui Checklist

- ☑ Lose the clutter—it's in the way of your energy.

- ☑ Think about where things will go before putting them there.

- ☑ Surround yourself with a variety of colors.

- ☑ Bring in healthy plants and flowers to generate positive energy.

- ☑ Fill your room with pleasurable smells for a healing effect.

- ☑ Avoid having naked walls— go for inspiration, instead.

- ☑ Use mirrors to make cramped spaces look and feel bigger.

- ☑ Play calming music to counteract stress and soothe the soul.

- ☑ Open your window to let in new chi.

- ☑ Hang a crystal in front of your window to bring in more color.

Get It Together

Have you ever had one of those days when you just can't find the one thing you really need? Hunting for that missing library book is no fun when the floor is covered in magazines and clothes. Finding that cute but lost tank top a season too late can be a real bummer, too.

Save yourself from that agony by getting it together—and getting organized! Make a list of your belongings, sorting them into categories. Start by taking on your closet. List your many pairs of shoes. Then decide which are keepers and which need to walk on out! After you've sorted through your closet, turn your attention to other areas of your room, like your desk and dresser.

What do you want to keep? What do you want to get rid of? You need to survey all your stuff and decide what stays or goes. Here are some questions you can ask yourself if you need help deciding:

Is It a Keeper or a Loser?

1. Is it something that is worth repairing?

2. How long has it been since you've used or enjoyed it?

3. How do you feel about the person who gave it to you?

4. Could you save a part of it (for memory sake) and lose the rest?

5. Is it something that would be better if used differently?

6. Would someone else get more use or pleasure out of it?

Top 10 Organization Tips

This section is for keepers only! Here's what you'll need to think about as you begin to put things away again:

1. Keep similar items together—especially socks! Label drawers and shelves accordingly.

2. Things you use frequently should be within easy reach.

3. Arrange your clothing in groups according to season, activity, or color.

4. Store clothes that don't fit—but you still want to keep—in a box.

5. Use baskets to store your knickknacks. At least they'll *look* organized!

6. Remember that you have space underneath your bed for storage. Flat boxes will work best.

7. Install some hooks on the inside of your closet door. Hang your belts, umbrellas, and purses.

8. Create a filing cabinet for all your paperwork. You can even color-code your folders to create a pretty filing system!

9. Keep a calendar where you can always see it. Write down important tasks and dates.

10. STAY ORGANIZED! Otherwise, you'll have to start all over again.

The Paint Shop

Is your room crying out for color? Repainting your walls is one way to give your room a *totally* different feel. However, that may be somewhat unrealistic—Mom and Dad might say no. But there are loads of things you *can* do with paint that will involve a lot less time and money—while still giving your room a new, colorful feel!

Sponge-Paint Furniture Fun

Is the paint on your old dresser chipping? Do you wish that your desk chair was pink instead of green? Ask your parents if you can give some of your furniture a paint job. Sponge painting is a great way to give your things a more colorful, whimsical feel.

You will need:

- Old sheet or large tarp
- Several soft cloth rags
- Some household cleaner (mild dishwashing soap or bubble bath)
- A bucket of water
- Medium-grade sandpaper
- A sponge that fits comfortably in your palm
- A couple of small cans of acrylic paint (in your colors of choice)
- Polyurethane finish (available at most paint stores)
- A foam brush

ASK FIRST

COLOR TIP

For lots of contrast, use colors in different hue families (light, medium, or dark). For less contrast, use colors in the same hue families.

Step 1: Lay an old sheet or a large tarp outside or in your garage (with the door open for ventilation).

Step 2: Clean the piece of furniture with a wet rag and some household cleaner (mixed in a bucket with some water).

22

Step 3: Use a piece of sandpaper to sand the piece in a circular motion. Be sure to sand the entire piece, but concentrate more on the edges of the piece than the flat area. Then, wipe away any dust with a rag.

Step 4: Wet the sponge and ring it out. Then dip a portion of the sponge into your base color paint. Squeeze it to get rid of excess paint.

Step 5: Lightly pat the sponge against the furniture's surface and apply the first coat of paint. Aim for evenness. (If you want a multi-colored look, leave room for the next color!)

Step 6: Once the base color is applied, wash the sponge. Allow the base coat to dry for one to two hours.

Step 7: If you will be using more than one color, dip your sponge in the second color and squeeze out any excess paint. Begin sponging all over, filling in new areas. Allow the paint to dry for two hours.

Visit
www.scholastic.com/makeover
to get cool color combination ideas from our color wheel!

Step 8: Once you're happy with the layers of paint, apply polyurethane finish with a foam brush. The more coats you apply, the shinier your piece will be. Allow 24 hours for each coat to dry.

Pat yourself on the back! You did an awesome job!

Terrific Tips

○ Be sure to wear rubber or plastic gloves on your hands to protect them while you work. Also wear old clothes—you wouldn't want to ruin any of your favorite items!

○ Begin sponging in the corners of the piece and then move your way into the center.

○ Press lightly with your sponge, or you might wind up with a patch that is too heavily painted compared to the rest.

○ Stand back occasionally to see which areas have enough paint and which still need more.

Paint a Pot!

Bring even more color into your room with a fabulous, painted pot! Just about any old container will do. A ceramic pot is ideal, but if you don't have one, grab an old coffee tin or large glass.

Be sure to choose colors that match your room's new color theme. And when it's finished, fill your new pot with flowers. Or just use it as a "neat" place to store all of your pesky knickknacks!

You will need:

- Old sheet or large tarp
- Paper towel and cleaning spray
- A clay pot or other container
- Empty garbage can
- Old newspaper
- Medium-sized foam brush
- Small cans of acrylic paint (in at least two colors)
- A roll of masking tape

ASK FIRST

Step 1: Set up shop outside or in your garage with the door open for ventilation—anywhere you're allowed to make a small mess! Once you've chosen your spot, lay down an old sheet or tarp to work on.

Step 2: Use paper towels and cleaning spray to clean your container.

Step 3: Sit the container atop a garbage pail that has been turned upside-down. (This way, you can move around the pot and see it from all angles while you're working.) Cover the pail with newspaper.

Step 4: Using your foam brush, paint the top half of your pot in one color and allow it to dry completely, which should take about 30 minutes. Note: If you are painting a can or tin, you will need to paint two to three coats of paint to cover the pre-existing design.

$\int tep$ 5: Adhere strips of masking tape to cover the bottom portion that has been painted. Make the tape as straight and even around the circumference of your pot as possible. This is important to protect your first layer of paint.

$\int tep$ 6: Paint the bottom half of your pot in a second color. Allow the paint to dry completely for about 30 minutes.

$\int tep$ 7: Remove the masking tape carefully to unveil your perfect pot!

Five Steps Farther!

O Make a grid pattern with your masking tape!

O Use lots of different colors for a funky finish!

O Try using more and less paint on your brush to create a shaded effect!

O Use a paintbrush and add details to your painted pot!

O Glue a piece of ribbon around the pot to give it a cute trim!

COOL COLOR COMBOS

The CHILL Chick — **BLUE & ORANGE**

The Free Spirit — **PURPLE & GOLD**

THE MODERN MAMA — **BLACK & SILVER**

The Pretty Princess — **PINK & PURPLE**

THE SUPER PREP — **NAVY & YELLOW**

The Flower Girl — **GREEN & ROSE**

Art Smarts

You probably didn't realize it, but you've got what it takes to make awesome artwork all by yourself! Here are some easy projects that you'll be proud to display when you're finished!

Starry Night

Most people don't decorate their ceilings. It's hard work to get up that high! But one thing you can do to fill that empty space is to make and hang a mobile!

You will need:

- Old newspaper
- A pencil with an eraser
- A large piece of poster board
- Ruler
- Scissors
- Hole-puncher
- Small paintbrush
- Craft glue
- Silver glitter
- Spool of string

Step 1: Cover your work space with old newspaper.

Step 2: Use your pencil to sketch a star on your poster board. It should be about 1-$\frac{1}{2}$ feet in length. Then, cut out the star shape and set it aside.

Step 3: Think about what shapes you want to hang from your mobile. (Make a mini galaxy by cutting out planets, moons, and smaller stars.)

Step 4: Sketch out the shapes you will hang on the remaining poster board and cut them out. Remember: Not all of your shapes need to be the same size.

Step 5: Count the number of shapes you will hang. Use the hole-puncher to punch that number of holes around the exterior of the giant star.

Step 6: Punch one additional hole on each of the tips of the large star.

Step 7: Use the hole-puncher to punch holes from the tops of the smaller shapes.

Step 8: Use your paintbrush to cover your large star with a thin layer of glue. Sprinkle glitter over the glue. Then turn the star upside down and shake off any extra glitter.

Step 9: Repeat the process with the smaller shapes. Cover each with glue, sprinkle the glitter, and then shake off any excess glitter.

Step 10: Cut pieces of string, one for each shape, each about 12 inches (one foot) in length. Note: The length can vary so that some shapes hang lower than others.

Step 11: Thread the string through the hole at the top of one of your small shapes and tie a knot. Then thread the other end of the string through an outside hole on your large star and tie another knot to secure it in place.

Step 12: Cut five more pieces of string, about 12 inches (one foot) in length each. Thread each through the holes at the star tips of the large star and tie a knot to secure the string to the star.

Step 13: Tie the five other ends of the string into one knot, which you will use to hang the mobile.

Ask an adult to hang your mobile, and prepare for the sweetest dreams you've ever had!

Do-It-Yourself Découpage

Découpage is the art of applying paper or fabric to a surface, and then covering that same surface with a clear finish (so everything stays put, of course!). Photographs, magazine clippings, old invitations, wrapping paper, postcards, notes and letters, handkerchiefs, and fabric scraps—almost any semi-flat material you feel inspired to use will work!

Did You Know? The word découpage is derived from the French word, decouper. Decouper means "to cut out."

You will need:

- Old newspaper or a tarp
- Scissors
- Lots of scraps and clippings
- A foam brush
- Poster board cut to the size you want
- Some découpage medium (Modgepodge is a popular brand that is available at most arts and crafts stores)

Step 1: Cover your workstation with newspaper or a tarp. Using scissors, cut your "motifs" (clippings and scraps) to the sizes you want them to be.

Step 2: Use the foam brush to cover your poster board with a layer of découpage medium.

Step 3: Carefully, arrange your motifs on the poster board. Overlap the edges of different pieces if you want to make your final poster look more interesting.

Step 4: When the motifs have been arranged and the poster board has been completely covered, apply a second coat of découpage medium over everything. Allow the finish to dry for 15 minutes.

Step 5: Apply one or two additional coats of découpage medium, allowing it to dry completely between new coats for 15 minutes.

Now your masterpiece is ready to be hung! (If you want to frame it first, turn to page 32 to learn how!)

Say It With Flowers

Tissue paper flowers are totally fun to make, and they look fantastic all year-round!

You will need:

- Multi-colored tissue paper (6 sheets per flower)
- Green pipe cleaners (2 per flower)
- Scissors

Step 1: Stack six sheets of tissue paper, one on top of the other.

Step 2: Accordion fold the stack of papers.

Step 3: Twist a pipe cleaner around the middle of the papers.

Step 4: Use scissors to cut the edges of the papers so they are slightly rounded.

Step 5: Gently lift each tissue layer, starting with the top layer, towards the center.

Step 6: Fluff the petals to make the flower look as lifelike as possible.

Step 7: Twist one end of the second pipe cleaner to the first, perpendicular to the flower, to make a stem.

Photo Fun

Nothing captures a moment like a photograph. One click of the camera and you can forever hold on to one split second in time. Don't be fooled by thinking that only professional photographers can take beautiful pictures. You can too!

Just think of a subject that means a lot to you—a person or animal that you love, a place that you enjoy visiting, even a self-portrait—and start snapping away!

If you don't own a camera, ask permission to borrow a family member's. If they don't have one to lend, you can buy a disposable camera at most convenient stores. Disposable cameras are pretty cheap and they take great pictures!

Hot Hangers
Hang your pictures with ribbons, magnets, and even clothespins (plain or decorated) to make your photo gallery more interesting!

CAN'T THINK OF WHAT TO PHOTOGRAPH?
Here are some ideas to get you started...

- Follow your pet around for some fun photo-opps!

- Take a family photograph —soft lighting will look best!

- Take individual portraits of each of your closest pals!

- Parks and gardens are perfect places for nature shots!

- Look around. Beauty is everywhere!

Create a Photo Gallery!

Now that you have all these wonderful photographs, what will you do with them? Create a photo gallery, of course!

Think about the way that you will arrange your photographs on your wall. How and where you hang these works of genius is an artistic statement in itself! Some artists like to cover their walls with their art, enjoying the opportunity to bask in their creativity. Others believe that just a photo or two per wall is sufficient—and that the selected pieces will get more attention if they are not competing against too many others. Which approach is more you?

Frame-azing

Most of the art you see on walls is flat, right? Make your wall special by hanging a dimensional box frame of your favorite belongings, instead!

You will need:

- Old newspaper
- A small paintbrush
- A shadowbox frame (available at craft stores and frame shops)
- A small container of acrylic paint (any color of your choice)
- Craft glue
- Glitter
- Memorabilia (an old key, a friendship bracelet, a lipstick container, a jelly bean, a secret note—anything that is significant to you!)
- Foam shapes

Step 1: Put down several layers of old newspaper to create your workstation.

Step 2: Use the small paintbrush to paint the box frame in a color of your choice. Wash the paintbrush and allow the paint to dry for about two hours.

Step 3: When the paint has dried, use the small paintbrush to spread a layer of glue around the border of the frame. Sprinkle some glitter over the glue. Then hold the frame up and shake off any extra glitter.

Step 4: Use more glue to make your favorite memorabilia stick to the inside of the frame. Stick your foam shapes onto the inside to give things a real 3-D effect!

Step 5: Assemble your shadowbox frame. Hang it somewhere where it will get all of the attention it deserves!

Freeze Frame!

Mount a photograph, a pressed flower—or anything you feel like hanging—in one of these super-simple frames!

You will need:

- A piece of thick cardboard (bigger than what you will be framing)
- X-Acto® knife
- Newspaper strips cut into rectangles (about 2" x 4" each)
- Clear craft glue
- Medium- and small-sized paintbrushes
- Small bottle(s) of acrylic paint (in your favorite colors)
- Small embellishments of your choice (glitter, confetti, beads, etc.)
- Clear tape
- A piece of string (Any kind of string will do, cut to about 4 inches in length.)

ASK FIRST

Step 1: Ask an adult to cut a rectangle from the inside of the cardboard piece using an X-Acto® knife. The outer portion will be your "frame" once the center has been removed. Note: The rectangle should be just a little smaller than the picture you will be framing.

Step 2: Cover the "frame" with your newspaper strips, gluing down the pieces. Layer the strips two to four more times. Allow the glue to dry, 15 minutes per layer.

Step 3: Using the medium-sized paintbrush, paint your frame in a solid color. You might need to paint more than one layer in order to cover up the newspaper fully (just wait for the paint to dry in between layers).

Step 4: Use the small-sized paintbrush to add details. (A vine trim is lovely on a pressed flower frame. Stars and hearts are perfect for frames that will hold photos of your best friends!)

Step 5: Use glue to add any embellishments you think will look nice. Sprinkle glitter or paste down beads to make the frame funky!

Step 6: Tape your picture to the back of the frame.

Step 7: Tie a small loop with your string and knot the end. Glue the end to the back of the frame.

Once the glue holding the string is dry, your frame is ready to be hung. Wow! It looks great!

Hang Around

Ask an adult to help you hang your new masterpieces. But before you do, remember that planning first always yields the best results. Make photocopies of what you will be hanging and tape the copies to the walls. Try them in different places. Be sure that you like the places you have chosen before you put holes in the wall!

FUN TIP

Did you know that your old CD cases make great mini-frames? Fill the case with filler, like paper or foam, and then place your photo in the center. Decorate the outside of the case with glitter glue or embossing pens!

Forever Flowers

Nothing says nature like fresh flowers. But, a flower won't last forever. Or can it? Pressing flowers is one way to keep a flower "alive" so that you can enjoy it for as long as you want.

You will need:

- Several fresh flowers (You will get the best results if you choose flowers that are in their early budding stage.)
- 2 coffee filters for each flower
- Several heavy books (Encyclopedias work really well!)
- Pair of tweezers
- Poster board cut to desired size (8-$\frac{1}{2}$" x 11" or smaller will look best)
- Small paintbrush
- Glue

Step 1: Place each flower between two coffee filters. (Coffee filters absorb moisture and will help speed up the drying process. They will also protect the pages in the book you will use.)

Step 2: Place the coffee-filter-wrapped flower between two pages of your heavy book. If you are pressing more than one flower at a time, be sure to leave several pages between each flower.

Step 3: Pile other heavy books and objects atop the book you are using for pressing.

Step 4: Wait for two weeks so that the flowers will truly be flattened and dry before you remove them. Be gentle when removing them. You may even consider using tweezers if the flowers or plants are especially fragile.

Step 5: Artistically arrange your pressed flowers on your poster board. Then remove them and use a small paintbrush to apply a layer of glue where you plan to put the flowers on the poster board.

Step 6: Press the flowers into the glue layer. Make sure as much of the flower or plant is touching the glue as possible. Allow it to dry completely for one hour.

Store that beauty somewhere safe and dry until you have a moment to frame it!

See pages 32-33 to learn how to frame your flower fantasy!

BEST WHEN PRESSED

Flowers with thin petals and blooms will look best when pressed. Try some of these!

Daisy

Freesia

Queen Anne's lace

Poppy

Buttercup

Herb

Fern

Beadazzling

Use beads to revamp your room! They come in all colors and sizes. Best of all, most beads are pretty inexpensive!

Curtain Call

Beadazzle all who enter your room by hanging a beaded curtain in the entrance! Note: After this curtain is hung, you won't be able to close your door. It's best for open doorways.

You will need:

- Measuring tape
- A spool of string or a ball of yarn
- Scissors
- An assortment of short, round beads (about 2 one-pound bags)
- A curtain rod or tension rod (available at most craft and hardware stores)

ASK FIRST

Step 1: Measure the length and width of your doorframe in inches. Write the measurements down. Note: You will want to hang one string of beads for every inch along your doorframe's width.

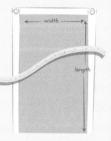

Step 2: Cut the number of pieces of string you will need. Each piece of string should be cut to the same measurement as the length of your doorframe.

Step 3: Thread the first bead onto a piece of string and tie a knot to secure the bead in place. You might need to double-knot the string to secure the bead—so check it.

Step 4: Continue threading beads until only about six inches of un-beaded string remain. Note: Count the number of beads you have used. This number is roughly the number of beads you will use for each remaining piece of string.

Step 5: Tie a knot above the last bead on the string. Use the remaining string to tie another knot and secure the beaded string to the tension rod.

Step 6: Repeat this process until you have beaded all of your pieces of string and hung them from your rod. Then ask an adult to hang the tension rod in your doorframe.

BEAD BASICS

Know your beads before you get started!

- **BUGLE BEADS:** Beads that are shaped like tubes

- **DROP BEADS:** Beads that are shaped like pears

- **FACETED BEADS:** Beads that have flat, patterned surfaces

- **"H" BEADS:** Beads that are usually in the shape of hexagons

- **PONY BEADS:** Beads that are shaped like circles or donuts

LINE IT UP!

Here's some *beadazzling* inspiration!

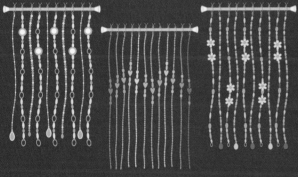

- Thread three colors and repeat the pattern as you thread the beads!

- Make a pattern based on the size of the bead you're using.

- Use the same type of bead for one string and a different one for the next!

Light 'n' Lovely

Create a beautiful, beaded shade for your bedside lamp!

Step 1: Lay some newspaper over your work space.

Step 2: Create a bead design for your lampshade. Will you line your beads on the bottom of the shade to give it a trim? Will you scatter them around for a more whimsical effect?

Step 3: Use your small paintbrush to apply glue to an area where you will be securing a bead. Hold the bead in the glue until it stays on its own. Repeat for each bead in your design.

Step 4: Let the shade dry for several hours before returning it to its base.

Stuck On You

Stamps are miracle-workers when it comes to turning the ordinary into extraordinary! Try one of these projects to spruce up your room!

Dream Garden

Tired of your plain sheets? Ask your parents if you can use fabric paint on your bedding. Then turn your solid-colored sheets into a field of flowers!

You will need:

- Lots of old newspaper or an old tarp
- Your sheet set (fitted sheet, top sheet, and pillow cases)
- A small paintbrush
- Flower sponge
- A jar or tube of fabric paint in your favorite color

ASK FIRST

Step 1: Lay down lots of newspaper or an old tarp outside or in your garage with the door open for ventilation. It should cover an area large enough so that one of your sheets can lay flat.

Step 2: Use the small paintbrush to cover one surface of the sponge in fabric paint.

Step 3: Press the sponge somewhere in the center of the sheet, creating a small, painted flower impression.

Step 4: Continue creating flowers all over the sheet, moving outward as you work so that the last areas you will work on are the edges. Use the small paintbrush to add more fabric paint to the sponge as needed.

Step 5: Repeat the stamping process with your other sheet and pillowcases.

Try using more than one color of fabric paint to make your flower sheets truly adorable!

Step 6: Be sure to allow the fabric paint to dry completely before making your bed again.

Potato Prints

Don't have a stamp with the design you want to use? Make your own stamp—with a potato! Then make a beautiful keepsake box for the things that are most special to you!

Step 1: Cover your work area with old newspaper.

Step 2: Use the foam brush to cover both the top and bottom of the shoebox with paint. Allow the paint to dry for two hours. Repeat this step if you feel the box needs an additional coat of paint.

Step 3: Clean the potato in water and dry it with a paper towel. Then ask an adult to use a kitchen knife to cut the potato in half.

Step 4: Use the felt-tipped pen to draw the shape you want on your potato (the flat face of the potato). Then have an adult use the craft knife to cut away the areas you don't want to show in your printing.

You will need:

- Old newspaper
- A foam brush
- An old shoebox
- Acrylic paint
- A potato
- Paper towel
- Kitchen knife
- Felt-tipped pen
- Craft knife
- Small paintbrush

ASK FIRST

Step 5: Now you're ready to stamp! Use the small paintbrush to paint the raised shape (only the area you want to show in your printing).

Step 6: Begin stamping the painted shoebox. Add more paint to the raised shape whenever the color begins to fade. Allow the paint to dry for two hours.

LINE IT UP!

Try using your new potato stamper on the items listed below. Liven them up with a colorful pattern!

- A trash bin
- A memo board
- A lampshade
- A jar

All that Glitters

Step 5: Sprinkle glitter over the glue. Then turn the switch plate upside down and shake it gently to remove any excess glitter. Allow the craft glue and glitter to dry for several hours.

Nothing makes a room sparkle more than glitter!

Switch It Up!

Change a boring switch plate into something spectacular by giving it a glittery finish!

Step 1: Cover your work area with old newspaper.

Step 2: Ask an adult to remove your switch plate from the wall.

Step 3: Use the small paintbrush to give the switch plate a coat of acrylic paint. Wash the brush and allow the paint to dry for two hours.

Step 4: Use the small paintbrush to cover the painted switch plate in a thin layer of glue.

You will need:
ASK FIRST
- Old newspaper
- A small paintbrush
- A jar of acrylic paint
- Craft glue
- Glitter
- Clear nail polish

Step 6: Apply a layer of clear nail polish to the switch plate. The polish will keep the glitter in place and give the switch plate a shiny finish. Allow the polish to dry for an hour.

Step 7: Ask an adult to return the switch plate to the wall.

CHECK IT OUT!
Take your glitter plate one step further!

- Cover some areas of your switch plate with masking tape to create a design!

- Sprinkle one layer in glitter and then add a little confetti before you apply the nail polish.

- Use glitter pens to draw illustrations and designs!

Look at You!

Mirrors are definitely useful. We depend on mirrors all the time —especially when we want to see how great we look! But most mirrors look pretty plain, don't they? Here's an easy way to glam up your mirror in minutes!

You will need:

- A plain mirror (any size)
- Measuring tape or a ruler
- A pencil with an eraser
- A sheet of graph paper
- Mini-adhesive gem stickers
- Adhesive foam shapes

Step 1: Measure the length and width of your mirror and write it down.

Step 2: Draw a smaller scale of your mirror on your graph paper. Use one box for every inch you counted.

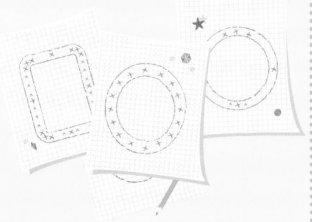

Step 3: Think about a pattern you will use to decorate the trim of your mirror. Will you alternate your stickers and foam pieces? Will you arrange them according to color, shape, or size? Count the number of gems and foam shapes you have, and count the colors and shapes they come in, too.

Step 4: Sketch the way your mirror will look when you're finished. Use your eraser to make changes. Keep sketching until you've got it right!

Step 5: Apply the decorations to the outer edge of your mirror, according to your plan.

Step 6: Step back and check it out—no, not yourself! The fine work you've done!

Now you'll have two reasons to feel proud when you look in your mirror — you look great and you're also an amazing artist!

41

Simply Scentsational

You've been working hard on that room of yours! Your room is looking fabulous. But does it smell as good as it looks?

Scents are important when you're setting a mood for your room. Here are some ways to give your room a sweet smell!

Perfect Potpourri

Potpourri is so easy to make you won't believe it!

You will need:

- Paper towel
- Fragrant flowers, herbs, or spices (Check out page 43 for some ideas!)
- Decorative materials to mix with flowers (wood shavings, twigs, pine cones, seeds)
- Medium-sized bowl
- Decorative pot or bowl
- Fragrance oils (You can find these at candle stores and organic food stores.)
- Spoon

Step 1: Spread out several sheets of paper towel and lay the plants and decorative materials on them to dry. Turn them every few days until they have dried completely.

Step 2: Separate the blooms and leaves from one another, and then mix them together in a bowl with your decorative materials. Transfer the mixture to a pretty pot or bowl. Note: If you haven't made enough potpourri to fill your pot, you can fill the bottom space with colorful tissue!

Step 3: Drop a few sprinkles of fragrance oil into the mixture and use a spoon to spread it around. Fragrance oils are very strong, so you won't need much to get the scent you want. You can add more drops every few weeks as the scent fades.

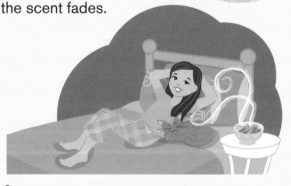

Step 4: Find a spot for your potpourri. Make sure that it is *not* underneath or in front of a fan or window, or your room will become one big potpourri mess! Also, keep it out of direct sunlight so the colors of your potpourri won't fade.

Simple Sachets

Make sachets out of your potpourri to give your clothes the same scent-sational smells!

You will need:

- Homemade potpourri
- A 6-inch square handkerchief or fabric square (Silk, cotton, or linen work best.)
- A piece of ribbon or string, about 6-inches in length

Step 1: Put a handful of potpourri in the center of a handkerchief.

Step 2: Tie the fabric corners together with a pretty string or ribbon.

Step 3: Place the sachet in your closet or dresser drawers.

Step 4: Every few months, squeeze the sachet to rejuvenate its scent.

Fun Facts

○ Fragrance oils can be found in the candle-making sections of most craft stores.

○ Pure fragrance oils are strong. Do not use too much at a time!

○ You can blend fragrance oils to create interesting combinations.

○ Fragrance oils are best stored in cool, dark places.

FRAGRANCE OIL FAMILIES

Family	Oils	
FLORAL	lavender, rose, violet, jasmine, and lilac	
FRUITY	berries, apple, mango, pear, peach, and coconut	
SPICY	cinnamon, nutmeg, vanilla, ginger, and clove	
CITRUS	orange, lemon, lime, grapefruit, and lemongrass	
HERBAL	peppermint, rosemary, sage, chamomile, and pine	
EARTHY	sandalwood, musk, honey, amber, and patchouli	

Party On

N ow that your room is looking oh-so-fabulous, you really need to show it off! What better way to do that then to throw a "room warming" party?

You're Invited

Ask your parents how many people you can invite over to check out your "new" room. Then give your friends a taste of your creativity by sending out these a-*door*-able invitations!

You will need:

- Heavy card stock
- Scissors
- Ruler
- Markers and gel pens (in variety of colors)
- Clear craft glue
- Glitter

ASK FIRST

Step 1: Cut out one card stock rectangle per guest. Each rectangle should be 10" x 8".

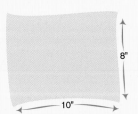

Step 2: Fold each rectangle in half, so the front measures 5" x 8".

Step 3: Use a marker to draw a doorknob on the front of the card, so the card resembles a door.

Step 4: In your best handwriting, use a gel pen to write, "Come on in!" somewhere on the door.

Step 5: Open the card and write the party info. Most important are the date, time, and address of your room-warming party!

Step 6: Add a P.S.: *Please bring a photo of yourself that I can keep and a wrapper from your favorite candy bar!*

It's A Party!
When? May 1st @ 3:30
Where? 5555 First St. Katie's Room
RSVP 555-5152
P.S. Please bring a photo of yourself & a wra...

Step 7: Close the card and draw a thin line of craft glue around the border. Sprinkle glitter over the glue, and then turn the card upside down so that any excess glitter falls off. Allow the glitter to dry for two hours.

Super-Cool Collage

Give your new space a friendly touch with one of these super-cool collages!

You will need:

- Old newspaper or tarp
- Photos of your friends
- Candy wrappers
- Several pairs of scissors
- Old magazines
- One standard poster board
- A small paintbrush
- Craft glue

Step 1: Cover your work area with old newspaper or a tarp. Gather the photos and wrappers your friends brought to your party.

Step 2: Give your friends old magazines and ask them to cut out captions they like.

Step 3: Arrange the photos, clippings, and wrappers on your poster board until you are all pleased with the way things look. Note: Overlapping the edges of items will give great results!

Step 4: Use the small paintbrush and craft glue to secure things in place. Allow the collage to dry for two hours.

Step 5: Decide with your friends where you will hang your new Friends Forever masterpiece. Then hang it!

COLLAGE COLLECTIONS

You can add lots of things to your Friends Forever collage. Try some of these ideas. Ask each of your friends to:

- make a color copy of the cover of her favorite book!
- each write a silly poem about what friendship means to her!
- write down her Top 10 memories with you!
- bring an illustration she has made specifically for the collage!

Quick Hits

Not feeling like you're ready to stop just yet? Wow, you are one energetic girl! Check out these 18 awesome interior decorating ideas you can try, too!

For the Pretty Princess

👑 Ask an adult to help you hang a silk or satin curtain above your bed in place of a headboard.

👑 Decorate clear CD cases with glitter and rhinestones and then use them to store your favorite pictures of your friends!

👑 Use two feathery boas (pink will look best, of course!) to tie back your window curtains.

For the Chill Chick

🕶 Use wire, string, and beads to fashion a dream catcher. Hang it in front of your window and rest assured that all of your dreams will be sweet ones!

🕶 Wrap a soft, old t-shirt around a small pillow and tie it closed with ribbon or string. How's that for a comfy spot for your head?

🕶 Collect beautiful shells and then spread them out on top of your windowsill. Now you can be at the beach all the time!

For the Super Prep

☀ Wrap a piece of tulle around a small pillow and tie the ends together with a pretty ribbon to create an adorable throw pillow!

☼ In your best handwriting and using your favorite pens, copy down favorite quotes and poems onto paper. Hang them around your room to enlighten your visitors!

☼ Decorate and fill lots of little frames with pictures of yourself and your family throughout the years. Arrange your new family tree atop a dresser!

For the Free Spirit

Give your mirror or memo board a funky trim with faux fur tape. Then hang all of your favorite clippings, notes, and itineraries.

Set an old trunk at the foot of your bed and use it to store extra blankets and pillows. Meanwhile, give the impression that an awesome adventure is on the horizon!

Hang different dangly earrings from the top rim of your lampshade to make it look funky!

For the Modern Mama

Use a Xerox machine to make reduced-sized color copies of your favorite photos. Glue magnets onto the backs to hang your memos in style!

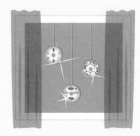

Decorate old CDs with glitter glue and hang them from clear wire in front of your window. Let everyone know whose room is really rocking!

For a modern piece of art, glue a variety of beads onto a sheet of paper in a pretty design. Then frame it!

For the Flower Girl

Use a découpage medium and a foam brush to cover a glass with pictures of flowers and then use it as a bud vase!

Hang a couple of floral air fresheners around your room to keep it smelling fresh!

Get a bunch of postcards of garden scenes and animals. Cover one or more of your walls with them to make your room feel like the outdoors!

P.S.!

You've been one busy girl! Look around your room—your hard work has really paid off! Your room looks so awesome it's hard to believe you did all this yourself, isn't it? You probably never even knew you had it in you!

But remember: Your taste will continue to change as you grow. The way your room looks now is perfect—but it might not look so perfect a year from now. That's why makeovers are so great. You can give your room a makeover again and again and again and again....

Wait a minute! Stop with the plans! You've done enough for the moment. For now, your job is a simple one: **Enjoy it!**